# I AM READING

# MRS HIPPO'S PIZZA PARLOUR

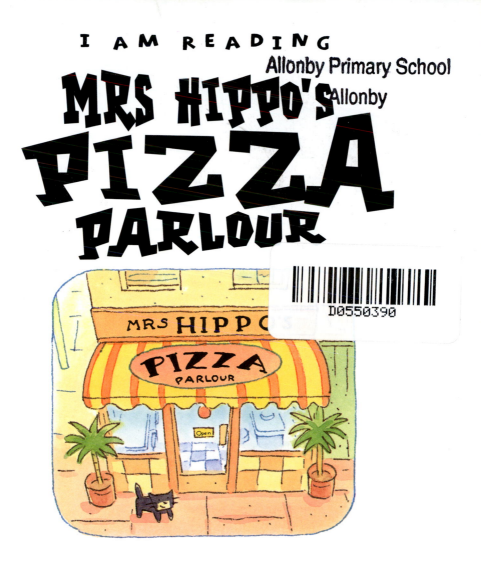

## VIVIAN FRENCH

*Illustrated by*
## CLIVE SCRUTON

MACMILLAN CHILDREN'S BOOKS

For all the lovely people at the Windsor Lodge Hotel  – V.F.
For my Nan, the best mince pie maker  – C.S.

First published by Kingfisher 1997

This edition published 2013 by Macmillan Children's Books
a division of Macmillan Publishers Limited
20 New Wharf Road, London N1 9RR
Basingstoke and Oxford
Associated companies throughout the world
www.panmacmillan.com

ISBN 978-0-330-51690-7

1 3 5 7 9 8 6 4 2

A CIP catalogue record for this book is available from the British Library.

Printed in China

# Contents

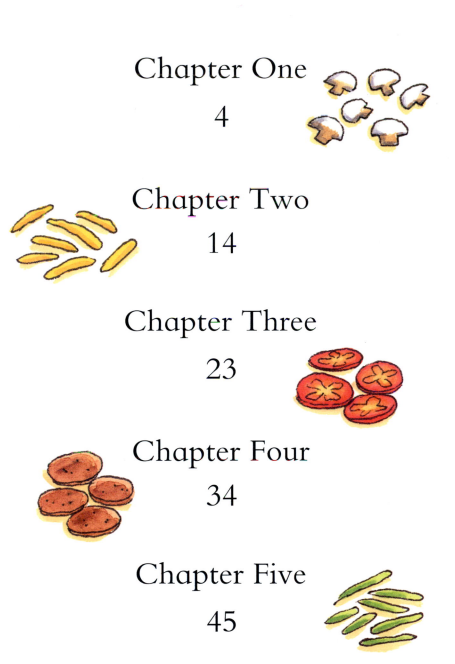

# Chapter One

It was two o'clock in the afternoon.

Mrs Hippo's Pizza Parlour

was empty.

Mrs Hippo was asleep.

William Hippo was reading

his comic. It was very quiet.

No one wanted to buy a pizza.

William put down his comic and
scratched his head.

He liked pizza.

His friends loved pizza.

So why didn't they come to

Mrs Hippo's Pizza Parlour?

Were they going somewhere

else instead?

Big Pig's Burger Bar gave away balloons.

Big Pig's Burger Bar had posters
all over town.

Maybe everyone was going there.

William's ears drooped.

If no one came to buy pizzas

there'd be no money.

No money meant no shopping . . .

and no shopping meant no bicycle

for William's birthday.

He'd seen a bicycle in the bicycle shop.

It was bright green, with a big bell.

William wanted that green bicycle.

He wanted it very badly.

RING!

It was the doorbell.

William ran to open the door.

"Hello!" said Ellie Bear.

"I've come to play!"

"Have you?" said William. "Why?"

Mrs Hippo opened one eye.

"Mother Bear's busy," she said.

"Come in, Ellie dear."

Ellie Bear took off her coat.

"Can I have a drink?" she asked.

William looked hopeful.

"Can we have biscuits, too?" he said.

"Two biscuits each," said Mrs Hippo.

"I haven't been shopping."

"Why not?" asked Ellie.

William leant towards Ellie.

"No one comes to buy pizzas any more,"
he whispered, "so we've got no money."

Mrs Hippo made hot chocolate
for Ellie and William.
She put four biscuits on a plate.
"Here you are, dearies," she said.
Then she went to make
herself a cup of tea.

Ellie drank her hot chocolate
very fast.
"I'm going to dunk my biscuits
in your chocolate," she told William.
She leant over the table . . .

William's hot chocolate spilt
everywhere.
"Oops!" said Ellie. "Sorry!"
William went to get a cloth.

When William came back the plate
was empty.

William put down the cloth with a
SPLATTT!

"Mum!" he yelled. "MUM!"

Mrs Hippo came hurrying in.

"What's the matter?" she asked.

"Ellie ate ALL the biscuits!"
said William.

Mrs Hippo looked at the mess.

"I think it's time we went out,"
she said.

"Let's go down to the sea."

"YES!" shouted Ellie and
William together.

# Chapter Two

At the back of the pizza parlour

was a little yard.

In the yard was a motorbike.

A gleaming, glittering motorbike . . .

with a bright red sidecar.

The wheels were shiny silver.

The handlebars were wide.

The horn was LOUD.

"WOW!" said Ellie.

"That's MUCH better than a bicycle!"

William didn't answer.

He wanted a bright green bicycle

which he could ride by himself.

"Helmets on!" said Mrs Hippo.

"And hop inside!"

BRRRRRRRRMMM!

Mrs Hippo revved up the motorbike.

"Hooray!" shouted Ellie.

"Go for it, Mum!" shouted William.

BRRRRRRRRRRRMMM!

They were off!

Down the road went the bike.
PARP! PARP!

They waved to little Tilly Tiger
and her dad at the bus stop.

17

Under the bridge.

PARP! PARP!

They waved to the Giraffe family
on their tricycles.

Right at the garage.
PARP! PARP!

They waved to the

monkey mechanics.

Left at the shops.

PARP! PARP!

They waved to Auntie Elephant.

Auntie Elephant was having

too much trouble with her

shopping trolley to wave back.

They zoomed on down to the sea.

"WHEEEEEEEEEEEEEEE!!"

yelled Ellie and William.

Mrs Hippo roared along the
sea road.

She roared over the promenade,
and down to the sand.

Then she stopped.

"WOW!" said Ellie, as she got out.

"That was FUN!"

# Chapter Three

"Now," said Mrs Hippo.

"What about making a sandcastle?"

"NO!" said Ellie. "I want to go for

another ride!"

"Me too," said William.

Ellie looked at the smooth yellow sand.

"Can we ride on the sand?"

she asked.

"Well . . ." said Mrs Hippo.

"There's no one here," said Ellie.

"We could make tracks!" said William.

Ellie jumped up. "We could write
ELLIE in the sand!"

"YES!" William jumped up too.

"EVERYONE will see it!" said Ellie.

"They'll see it on the moon!"

Ellie and William rushed back
into the sidecar.

Mrs Hippo climbed onto the
motorbike.

BRRRRRRRRRRRMMM!

They were off.

First of all they wrote ELLIE

in the sand.

"That's good," said Ellie. "Now

write William."

"No," said William.

"Why not?" asked Ellie.

"I've had an idea," William said.

His eyes were shining.

"An idea about the pizza parlour!

It's a MUCH better idea than

Big Pig's posters!"

He whispered in Mrs Hippo's ear.

Mrs Hippo nodded . . .

"Write it BIG, Mum," William told her.

Mrs Hippo got ready.

BRRRRRRRRRRRRRMMM!!

Right across the sand they roared.

Up and down,

and round and round.

At last Mrs Hippo stopped.

They all looked at the sand.

"WOW!" said Ellie.

"'MRS HIPPO'S PIZZAS ARE
THE BEST!'"

"EVERYONE will see that!" William
said happily. "They won't want to go
to Big Pig's Burger Bar now."

"They'll see it for ever and ever!"
said Ellie.

"No, dearie," said Mrs Hippo.

"The tide will come in tonight.

It will wash the sand all clean and

smooth again."

"Oh," said Ellie. Then she smiled.

"We could do it again tomorrow!"

"Maybe," said Mrs Hippo.

"But now we'd better be going home."

"Can we have an ice cream?"

asked Ellie.

Mrs Hippo shook her head.

"I'm sorry, dearie," she said.

"Look! Not even a penny in my purse!"

William looked sad again.

He thought about his birthday.

They'd have to sell lots and LOTS
of pizzas to make enough money for
a green bicycle.
A bright green bicycle with a big bell.
"What's the matter, William?"
asked Ellie.
"Nothing," said William.
"We'll go home the long way,"
said Mrs Hippo. "That'll cheer us all up!"

# Chapter Four

It was five o'clock when they
got home.

"Mum!" said William.

"Look at all those people outside
our Pizza Parlour!"

"Dear me," said Mrs Hippo.

"I think they're waiting to come in!"

"What do they want?" asked Ellie.

"PIZZAS!" said William.

"HOORAY!"

They all hurried inside.

"Come on, Ellie!" said William.

"We've got things to do!"

"I'll help," said Ellie. "I like helping!"

Mrs Hippo lit the oven.

Then she grated the cheese . . .

and cut up the onions . . .

and sliced the mushrooms . . .

and diced the peppers.

William rolled out the pizza dough.

And Ellie helped, too.

She tidied the tables . . .

and brushed the floor . . .

and shook the ketchup bottle  . . .

SPLATT!!

"Ellie," said Mrs Hippo.

"Yes?" said Ellie.

Mrs Hippo took away the ketchup bottle.

"Wouldn't you like to read William's comic?"

"No," said Ellie. "I like helping."

39

At half past five Mrs Hippo opened
the pizza parlour door.

"Do come in," she said.

"We saw your sign on the sand,"
said Tilly Tiger.

"So did I!" said Auntie Elephant.

"We did, too!" said Grandpa Giraffe.

"Don't want burgers any more!"
said Baby Giraffe.

"We love pizza!" said the monkeys.

"That's right!" everybody said.

"We LOVE pizza!!"

Mrs Hippo and William
worked and worked.
Ellie went on helping.

At half past seven Mother Bear came
into the pizza parlour.
"Oh my!" she said. "You ARE busy!"
"Yes," puffed Mrs Hippo, "we are!"
Ellie gave her mother a big hug.
"We wrote, 'Mrs Hippo's Pizzas
are the Best!' in the sand and now
everybody's come to see!"

"YES!" said Willliam. "And they all want LOTS and LOTS of pizzas!"
Mrs Hippo nodded. "Tomorrow I'm cooking a new Seaside Special! – so they're all going to come back, and bring their friends!"
"Goodness!" said Mother Bear.

"We'd love to see Ellie again,"
said Mrs Hippo. "What about Sunday?"

"That's my birthday!" said William.

"That's right," said Mrs Hippo.

"Ellie can come for birthday tea

and see your present!"

And she winked at Ellie, and gave

William a big hug.

# Chapter Five

On Sunday, Ellie rang the doorbell.

RING!

William opened the door.

"Hi!" said Ellie. "Where's your

present from your Mum?"

"Come and see," said William.

And there in the middle of the

pizza parlour was . . .

the bright green bicycle with a big bell.

And what did they have for tea?

SPECIAL BIRTHDAY PIZZA!!!

## About the Author and Illustrator

**Vivian French** used to be an actor. She has written lots of books for children and often visits schools and libraries to tell her stories. She and Clive Scruton have been friends for a long time. They first thought up the story of *Mrs Hippo's Pizza Parlour* while sitting together on a beach . . . eating pizza! Vivian French's other books include *Tiger and the Temper Tantrum* and *Tiger and the New Baby*.

**Clive Scruton** wanted to be either Spiderman or a cosmonaut when he was a child. But then he discovered he could draw – and has since illustrated over fifty books for children. Now he is married and lives in a house surrounded by his children, their rabbits and his own comics and robots. Clive often goes on bicycle rides . . . but what he really wants is a bright red motorbike with a sidecar!

If you've enjoyed reading *Mrs Hippo's Pizza Parlour,*
try these other **I Am Reading** books:

ALLIGATOR TAILS AND CROCODILE CAKES
Nicola Moon & Andy Ellis

BARN PARTY
Claire O'Brien & Tim Archbold

GRANDAD'S DINOSAUR
Brough Girling & Stephen Dell

JJ RABBIT AND THE MONSTER
Nicola Moon & Ant Parker

KIT'S CASTLE
Chris Powling & Anthony Lewis

MISS WIRE AND THE THREE KIND MICE
Ian Whybrow & Emma Chichester Clark

MR COOL
Jacqueline Wilson & Stephen Lewis

PRINCESS ROSA'S WINTER
Judy Hindley & Margaret Chamberlain

WATCH OUT, WILLIAM
Kady MacDonald Denton